The Book That I Love To Read

STORY BY JOE FITZPATRICK

ILLUSTRATIONS BY MARK KUMMER

Hi.

Welcome to my book . . .

Ya, I know, in a way this is your book, too,
but this is really MY book,
because this is THE BOOK THAT I LOVE TO READ!

I KNOW what you are thinking,
"Maybe this is the book that I love to read, too!"

Well, MAYBE it is, but have you ever had a book that was your FAVORITE book?

A book you take with you wherever you go?
If you were me, then that book is this book, because this is

THE BOOK THAT I LOVE TO READ.

Do you think it might be the book that you love to read?
Well . . . there is only one way to find out. You know what that is?

READ IT!

COLORS!

ALL KINDS of colors. There is ORANGE over there, RED right here, PURPLE is around here somewhere - do you see it?

Yellow

Magenta

Blue

Purple

Tangerine Fuchsia Orange Red Green Aquamarine

This book doesn't stop at regular colors. It even has weird ones, like AQUAMARINE, TANGERINE, MALACHITE, and even FUCHSIA - which I know is really pink, but it is much cooler when you say FUCHSIA. You know what ELSE this book has?

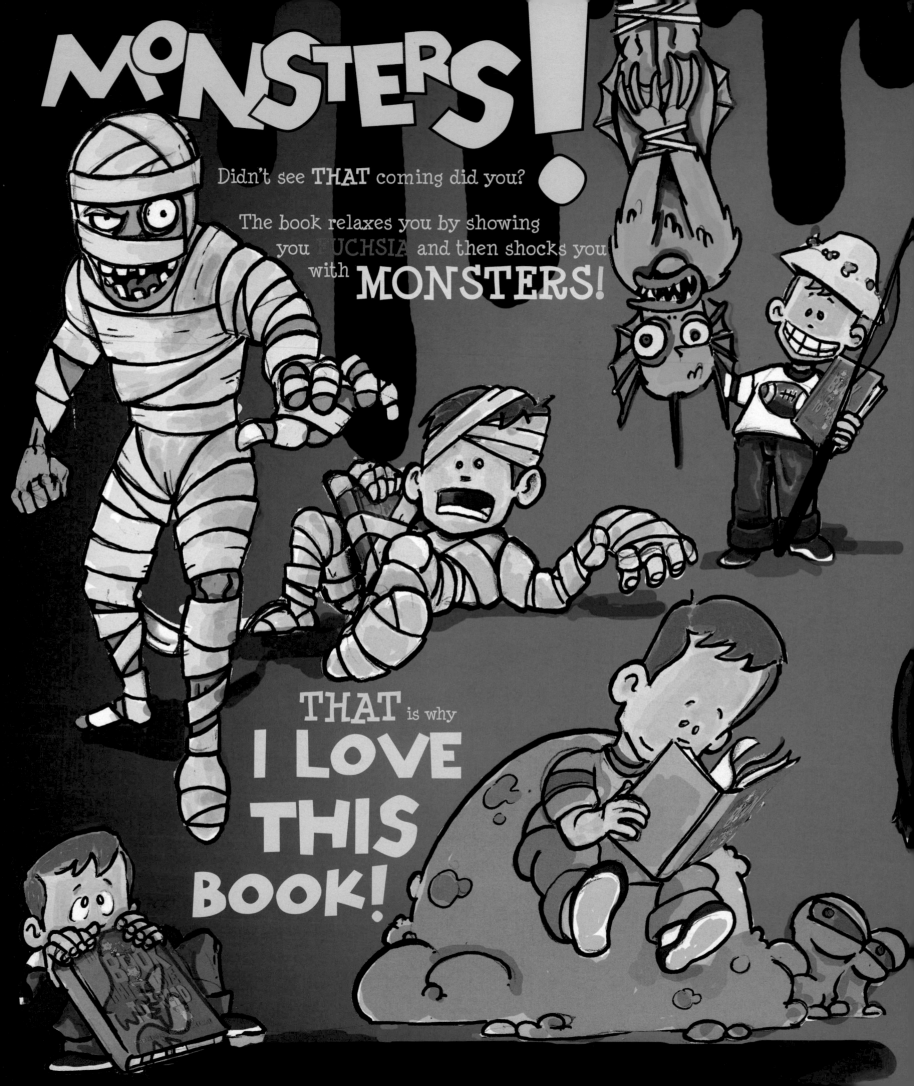

SOMETIMES when I read it I am **scared** of the MONSTERS.

SOMETIMES I am **friends** with the MONSTERS.

SOMETIMES I **fight** the MONSTERS.

SOMETIMES when I read this book I **AM** the MONSTERS.

This book is AWESOME!

You know why else I love this book?

DOLLS! DOLLS

WAIT a MINUTE... how did my little sister get in MY book?!?

This book DEFINITELY

*Sorry for any confusion this may have caused.

There are **NO** DOLLS in **this** book.

?!?!

does **NOT** have dolls!*

You know what there ARE?

These aliens like playing all kinds of **cool games** and **sports**, but their very FAVORITE sport to play is **ALIEN TACKLE FOOTBALL**. Alien tackle football is **really** hard, but I am **really** good.

Whenever we pick teams for alien tackle football, I am ALWAYS the first one picked. That is because I am the BEST alien tackle football player in this WHOLE BOOK.

CRUNCH
CRUNCH

Achoooooo

BOING BOING BOING

BEEP BEEP

OOF

Ya, I **KNOW**, cool word **right**?
What this word means is that a word
SOUNDS like the **sound** that it describes,
like **BANG** or **CLICK**.
This book has these kinds of words **all**
over these pages. Try saying them.
It is **SO** fun. Try and make them sound
like the sound they describe . . .

**FUN
RIGHT?**
Want to know
another cool
word about
words?

ALLITERATION.

(Say A-Lit-Ur-A-Shun)

This is **another** cool word.
It is also a **cool** thing when you see it in books.
It means that a BUNCH OF WORDS TOGETHER
start with the **same** letter, like **these** . . .

CRAZY CARTOON CHARACTER
CARRIES CUCUMBERS

BiG BOY BOUNCES BALL BEHiND BUS

SUPER SURFER SHOWS
SWEET SKILLS

PURPLE PERSON
PLAYS PING PONG

Alliteration is pretty cool and often silly. This book has alliteration in it.
That is **another** reason why this is
THE BOOK THAT I LOVE TO READ!
This book is silly. And I LOVE . . .

SILLY!

This book can be **REALLY** silly.
Just LOOK AROUND this page.
Silly right?

Don't get TOO comfortable because this book is also . . .

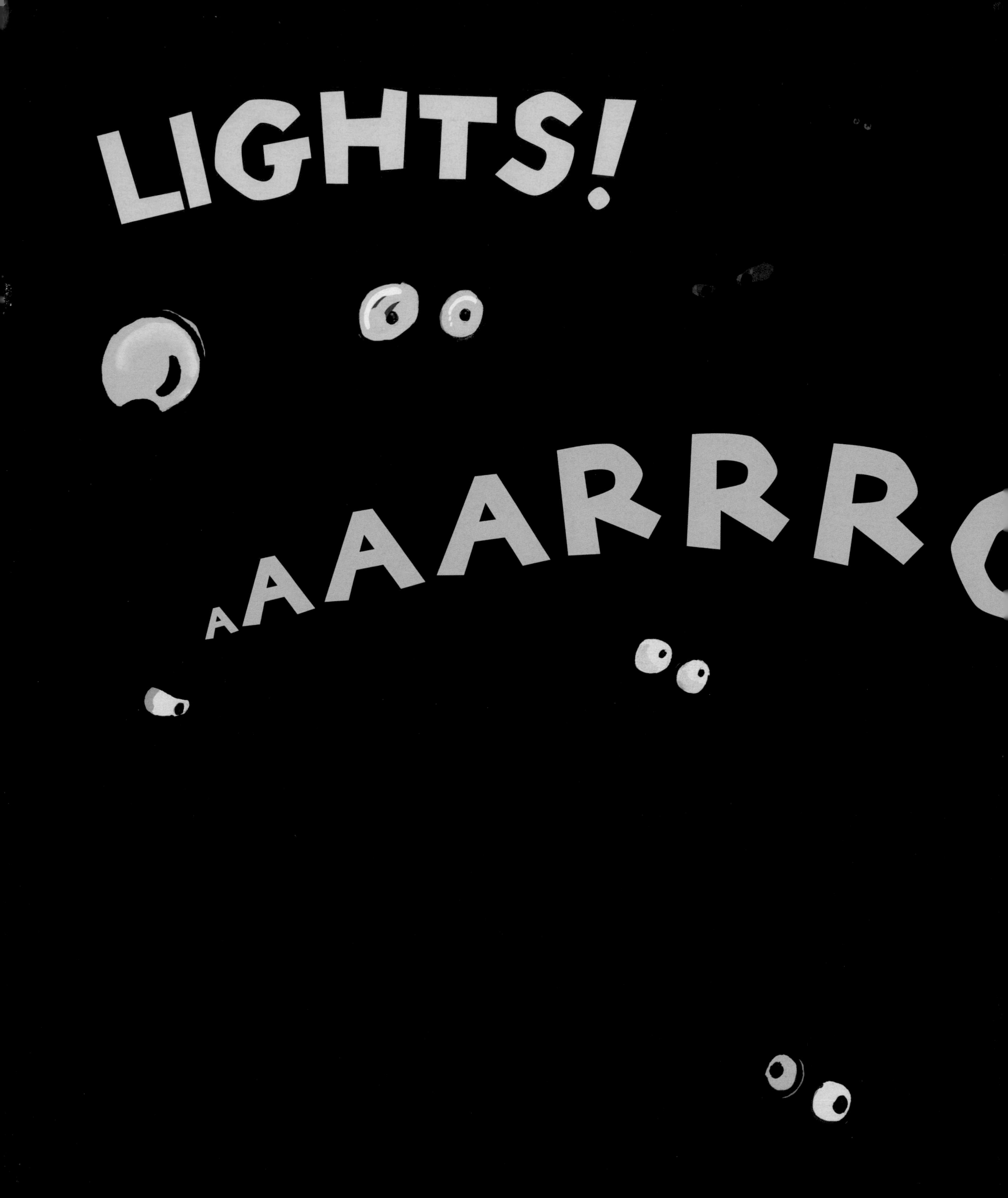
LIGHTS!
AAAARRR

GGHH!!!

TURN THE LIGHTS BACK ON!

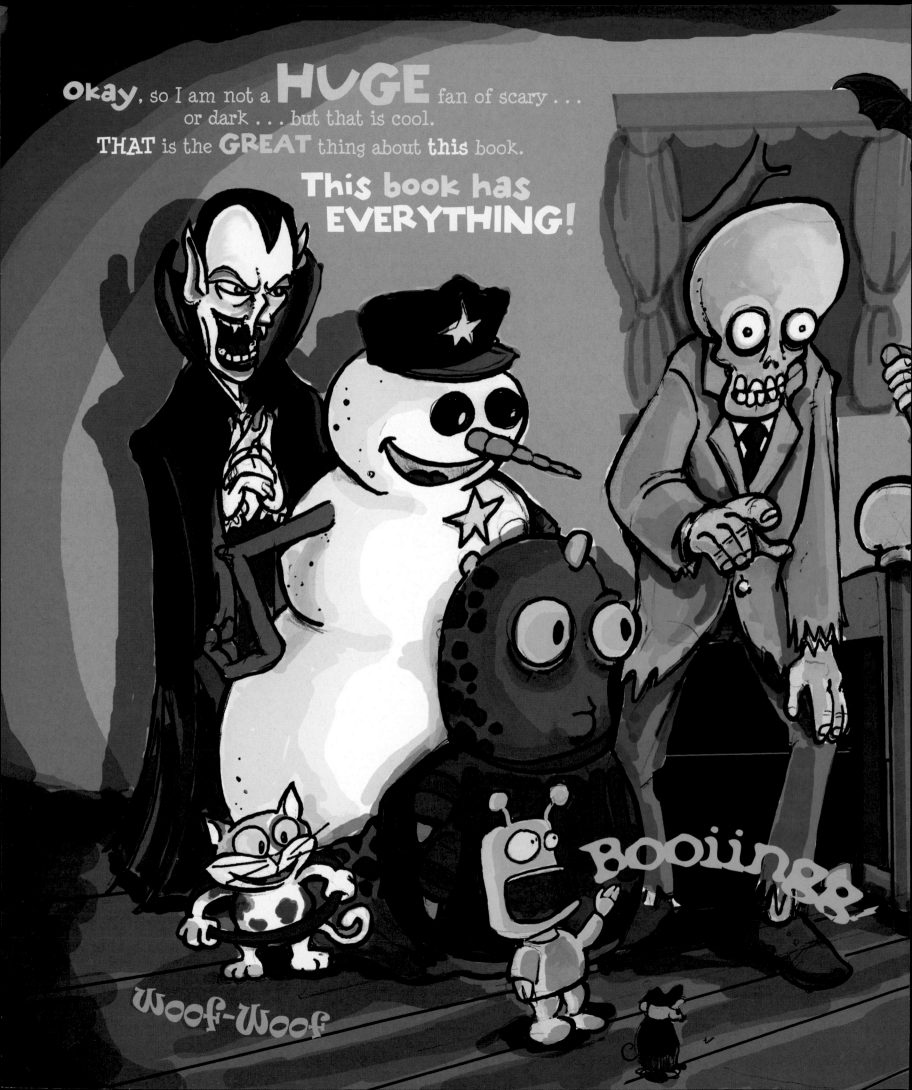

So if **scary** and **dark** is your thing,
then it is in here.
If **SILLY** is your thing, then it is in here.
If you like **PiRATES**,
or **MONSTERS**, or **ALIENS**,
or **alliteration**, it is all in here.
And so this is **THE BOOK THAT I LOVE TO READ.**

THAT is it.
THAT is my book. THIS is my book.

Do you dig it?

Do you have a favorite part?

Is the WHOLE thing your favorite part?

Can you now say, "This is **THE BOOK THAT I LOVE TO READ!?!**"

I hope so. If it is MAYBE we can share this book.
In fact, MAYBE I will let you have this book.

MAYBE.

But you are going to have to **catch** me first . . .